More than anything in the world, Little Porcupine wants a part in the Baby in the Manger play. But Cub Bear, Kit Squirrel, Piggy, and the rest of the Little Creatures think he's much too funny looking even to try out. "A stick ball like you?" they hoot. "You can be the stage crew. You can pick up dirty tinsel with your spines."

Little Porcupine runs home. Tears roll down his spiny cheeks. Mama Porcupine gives him a big pinchy hug. "You are not funny looking," she says. "Your spines shine. Your eyes sparkle. You are the light of my life."

But it is not until the night before Christmas, the very night of the Baby in the Manger play, that little Porcupine sees the truth in his mother's words.

How Little Porcupine Played Christmas

How Little Porcupine Played Christmas

by Joseph Slate

illustrated by Felicia Bond

Thomas Y. Crowell   New York

Text copyright © 1982 by Joseph Slate
Illustrations copyright © 1982 by Felicia Bond
All rights reserved.
Printed in the United States of America.
No part of this book may be used or reproduced
in any manner whatsoever without written permission
except in the case of brief quotations
embodied in critical articles and reviews.
For information address Thomas Y. Crowell Junior Books,
10 East 53rd Street, New York, N.Y. 10022.
Published simultaneously in Canada
by Fitzhenry & Whiteside Limited, Toronto.

Library of Congress Cataloging in Publication Data

Slate, Joseph.
How little porcupine played Christmas.
Summary: Even though the other animals exclude him
from the Christmas play because of his quills, Little
Porcupine still ends up in a starring role.
[1. Christmas–Fiction.   2. Animals–Fiction]
I. Bond, Felicia, ill.   II. Title.
PZ7.S6289Ho   1982   [E]   81-43884
ISBN 0-690-04237-X   AACR2
ISBN 0-690-04238-8 (lib. bdg.)

10 9 8 7 6 5 4 3 2 1
FIRST EDITION

For the Godchildren—
Cassidy, Cathy, Jonathon, John,
Kevin, Kris, Mark, Marty,
Philip, Richard, Shannon, Steve,
Tim, and Wally.

It is time for the Christmas play.

Little Porcupine gives his mother

a big ouchy hug.

"Oh, Mama, I would so like a part," he says.

"Then you must try out," says Mama Porcupine.

Little Porcupine looks in his mirror.

He pops his spines. He crosses his eyes.

He stands on one foot.

"But I am too funny looking," he says.

"I don't have red hair like Fox.

I don't have long ears like Bunny.

And I don't have webbed feet like Duckling."

Mama Porcupine gives Little Porcupine
a big prickly hug.
"You are not funny looking," she says.
"Your spines shine. Your eyes sparkle.
You are the light of my life."

"The light of my life!"
Little Porcupine loves his mother's words.
He runs off to school.
There, the little creatures are lined up
for parts in the Baby in the Manger play.
"My turn to try out," says Little Porcupine.

"No," says Little Fox. "There is
no part for you in the play.
You are too funny looking."

"Besides," says Chipmunk, "the cotton
snow will stick to your spines."
"And so will the tinsel," says Bunny.

"You can be the stage crew," says Cub Bear.

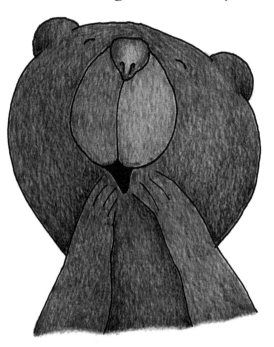

"You can be the cleanup crew," says Mouse.

"Yes, you can pick up dirty tinsel
with your spines," says Kit Squirrel.

"And put the tinsel in the trash," says Piggy.

"I don't mind being the stage crew,"
says Little Porcupine. "I don't mind
being the cleanup crew. But, oh,
I would so like a part
in the Baby in the Manger play."

"What part?" asks Duckling. "I suppose
you want to play the Little Baby.
Shame! A stick ball like you!"
"Stick Ball! Stick Ball!"
the little creatures laugh and hoot.

"Oh, no," says Little Porcupine shyly,
"I—I didn't mean I wanted the *best* part."
"Then what part do you think
you could play?" asks Possum.
"I could be a Shepherd and carry Lamb."
"Oh, no," says Lamb.
"Your spines would stick me."
"I could be a Wise Man and carry a gift box."
"Oh, no," says Chick. "Your spines
would punch the gift full of holes."
"I could be a King with a pointy crown."
"Oh, no!" says Raccoon.
"Your pointy body would hide the crown."
"Stick Ball! Stick Ball!"
Little Porcupine runs home.
Tears roll down his spiny cheeks.

"I am just a stick ball,"
he says to his mother.
"No, no," says Mama Porcupine.
She gives him a big pinchy hug.

"You are the light of my life.
And you will be the best stage crew
and the best cleanup crew
the little creatures ever had."

Four days before Christmas,
all the little creatures have a part.
All but Little Porcupine.

Three days before Christmas,
all the little creatures have a costume.
All but Little Porcupine.
Two days before Christmas,
all the little creatures
know where to stand on the stage.
All get to stand on the stage
but Little Porcupine.
Now it is the night before Christmas,
the night of the Baby in the Manger play.

"Fix the tree, fix the tree,

Stick Ball," say the little creatures.

Little Porcupine runs behind the manger.

He sets up the pine tree.

"Clean up, clean up, Stick Ball."

Little Porcupine picks up all the fallen

tinsel and sticks it on his spines.

"We are ready, we are ready,

Stick Ball," say the little creatures.

Little Porcupine peeks through the curtain.

The Mamas and Papas are in their seats.

He turns down the house lights.

He turns up the stage lights.

He pulls the curtain rope.

The curtain opens.

Here is the Baby in the Manger.

And here are the Mamas and Papas
in their seats.
They look at the little creatures.
"Ahhhhhhh," say the Mamas.
"Ohhhhhhh," say the Papas.

"But where is the star in the sky?"
say the Mamas.
"The Wise Men need to follow a star
to the Baby in the Manger,"
say the Papas.

"Oh, dear!
Oh, my!
Oh, help!"
cry the little creatures.

"I will help," says Little Porcupine.

"I will find a star."

He runs behind the manger.

He climbs the pine tree.

"Oh, what a beautiful star," say the
Mamas and the Papas.
"Star! Star!" say the little creatures.
"Star of my life," says Mama Porcupine.

And it is true.

Above all the others,

Little Porcupine is a shiny

spiny

star.